D0183939

This Little Tiger
book belongs to:

_____

_____

_____

529 692 54 6

Especially for two Anitas, with love
~ M C B

For my niece Stephanie Bahrani
~ T M

LITTLE TIGER PRESS
1 The Coda Centre,
189 Munster Road, London SW6 6AW
www.littletiger.co.uk
First published in Great Britain 2015
This edition published 2016
Text copyright © M Christina Butler 2015
Illustrations copyright © Tina Macnaughton 2015

M Christina Butler and Tina Macnaughton have asserted
their rights to be identified as the author and illustrator of this
work under the Copyright, Designs and Patents Act, 1988

A CIP catalogue record for this book is available from the British Library
All rights reserved • ISBN 978-1-84869-130-8
Printed in China • LTP/1800/1442/0516
2 4 6 8 10 9 7 5 3 1

One Snowy Rescue

M Christina Butler • Tina Macnaughton

LITTLE TIGER PRESS
London

"Gracious me!" cried Little Hedgehog, pushing at his door. "It must have snowed all night and now my house is in the middle of a snowdrift! However am I going to get out?"

With a wriggle,
Little Hedgehog pulled
himself through his window
and fell . . .

Splat!

into a big heap
of snow.

"Phew! I've never seen snow so deep," he gasped.

Once he'd cleared his path, Little Hedgehog sat down to rest. "Oh my!" he thought, all of a sudden. "I hope Mouse isn't snowed in too. I'd better go and see if she's all right."

Little Hedgehog set off carefully
towards Mouse's house.
    But the snow was very
deep for a small hedgehog
and suddenly he tumbled
into an enormous
snowdrift.

"Oooohhh!"

Slipping and sliding,
Little Hedgehog tried
to climb out of the hole.
But each time he landed
on his bottom . . .

Flump!

"Oh dear!" he thought.
"Whatever shall I do?"
But then he had a
wonderful idea.

Little Hedgehog popped his
hat on the end of his stick and
waved it about like a flag!

"What on earth is that?"
said Rabbit, who was
hopping by. "Hang on!
I've seen that hat before!"

"Little Hedgehog!" he called.
"What are you doing down there?"
    "I'm stuck, Rabbit! Can you
help me out?" a little voice
shouted back.

And with a big *"Heave-ho!"*
Rabbit pulled Little Hedgehog
out of the hole.

"I was on my way to see if Mouse and the
babies were all right," Little Hedgehog said.
"I'll come with you," said Rabbit.
So off they went, plod, plod, plodding
through the thick snow, as the snowflakes
swirled around them.

On and on they went until they came across some footprints.

"Hmm," said Rabbit, twisting his whiskers. "These are rabbit prints!"

"And these are hedgehog prints," cried Little Hedgehog. "Oh, Rabbit! Do you think these are *our* footprints?"

"If they are," replied Rabbit, "we are well and truly lost!"

The two friends trembled as the cold wind whistled through the trees and the snow grew deeper and deeper.

Just then a loud voice made them jump.
"What are you doing out in this weather?"
It was Fox!

"We're trying to find Mouse's house," said
Little Hedgehog.

"And now we're lost!" cried Rabbit.

"I can show you the way," said Fox.
And they set off towards the river.

They had not gone far when the snow
began to crumble under their feet.

"Help!" they cried, clinging to the riverbank
as the icy water rushed beneath.

"Ooh! I've dropped my hat!" Little Hedgehog
squeaked.

Then quick as a flash, Badger was above them. One by one, he pulled his friends onto the path. "I knew you were in trouble," he cried. "I saw your hat floating down the river!"

"Oh thank you!" gasped
Little Hedgehog. "I thought
I'd lost it forever."

With Fox leading the way, it wasn't
long before they found Mouse's
house. Everyone worked as fast
as they could to clear the snow.

"Am I glad to see you!" squeaked
Mouse when at last she could open
her door. "Thank you, everybody!"
"Well," laughed Badger. "I've
seen enough snow to last me a
lifetime! Let's go home for supper."

"Look at these little mice, cosy and snug in your hat!" chuckled Badger. "Whatever would we do without it?"

Little Hedgehog sighed happily. "And whatever
would we do without our friends?"
Then, by the soft silver light of the moon,
they chatted and giggled all the way home.

More terrific tales of friendship and fun from Little Tiger Press!

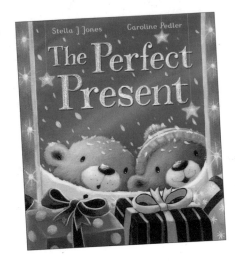

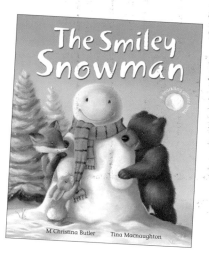

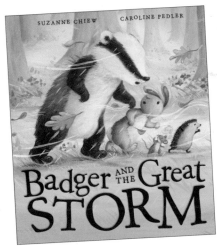

For information regarding any of the above titles
or for our catalogue, please contact us:
Little Tiger Press, 1 The Coda Centre,
189 Munster Road, London SW6 6AW
Tel: 020 7385 6333
E-mail: contact@littletiger.co.uk
www.littletiger.co.uk